Originally published in France in 2004 by Éditions du Seuil under the title *Garçon Fille / Fille Garçon*.
Copyright © 2004 Éditions du Seuil. Original ISBN 2-02-062085-5.
English edition copyright © 2004 Éditions du Seuil.

Manufactured in Belgium.
ISBN 2-02-067608-7.
Library of Congress Cataloging-in-Publication Data available.

Distributed in Canada by Raincoast Books
9050 Shaughnessy Street, Vancouver, British Columbia V6P 6E5

10   9   8   7   6   5   4   3   2   1

Chronicle Books LLC
85 Second Street, San Francisco, California 94105 • www.chroniclekids.com

BOy

meets girl

V. RADUNSKY

seuil chronicle

Boy

Boy

keep reading • • • even if you have to stand on your head!

meets

meets

green

nothing

We nothing

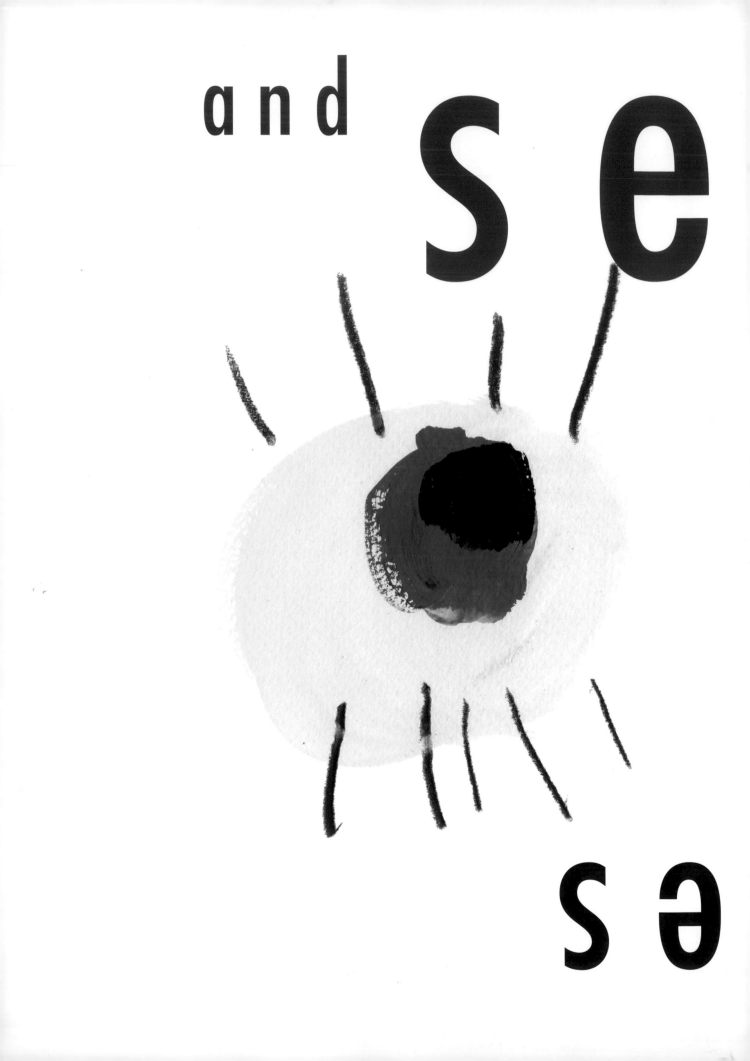

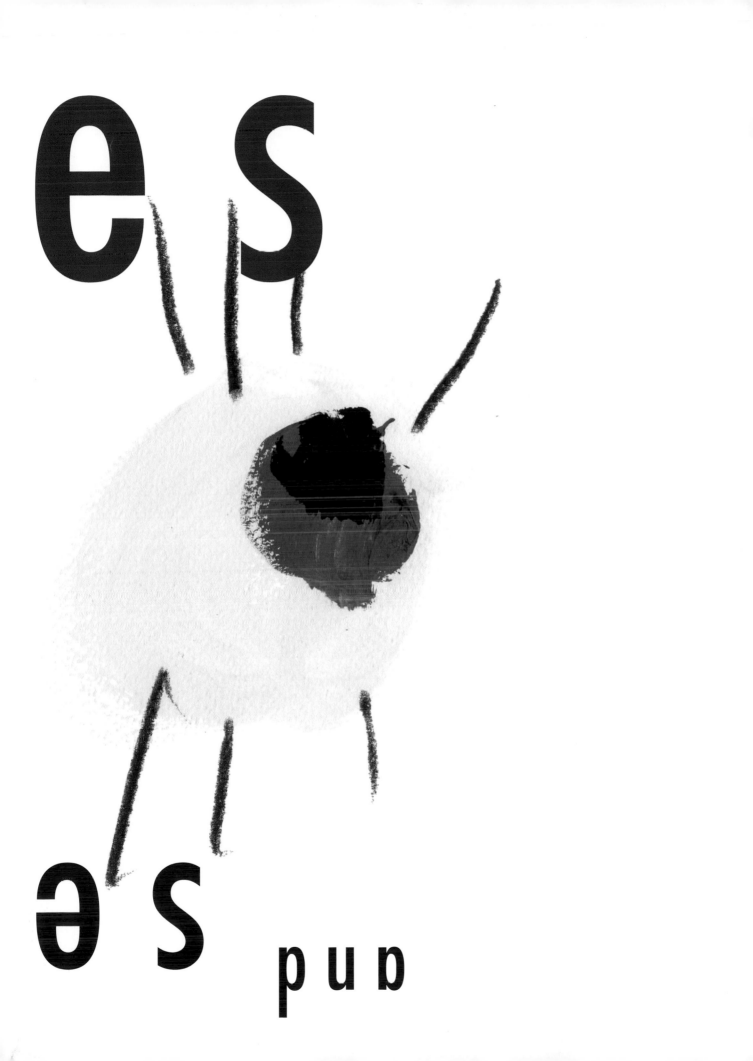

table

U

table

nder

under

glasses **we**

glasses **we**

aring

gnir

wearing

red

meets

meets

girl
meets boy

C. RASChKA

seuil ∞ chronicle